If I Had A Baby
written and illustrated by
Alanna Grayce Campbell

Copyright © 2024 by Alanna Grayce Campbell
All rights reserved.
Printed in the United States of America
First Edition

Illustrations © by Alanna Grayce Campbell
Cover art © by Alanna Grayce Campbell
Library of Congress Control Number: 2024919146

Publisher's Cataloging-in-Publication Data
Campbell, Alanna Grayce, 1995-
    If I Had a Baby / by Alanna Grayce Campbell; illustrated by Alanna Grayce Campbell. Niceville, Florida : Bohannon Hall Press, 2024.
    24 p. : color illustrations; 22 cm.

"A favored aunt dreams about having her own children."

1. Juvenile fiction. 2. Illustrated children's books. 3. Family life—Fiction. I. Title. II Campbell, Alanna Grayce, 1995-
PZ7.1C36 I3 2024   813.6 C36 I3   2024919146

ISBN 978-1-962995-05-4 (softcover)
ISBN 978-1-962995-06-1 (hardback)

PUBLISHED BY BOHANNON HALL PRESS

for Emma, Chloe, and Jameson—
I am so proud to be your aunt.
If I had a baby,
I hope they'd be like you.
Alanna ♡

If I had a baby, I hope that they'd be kind.

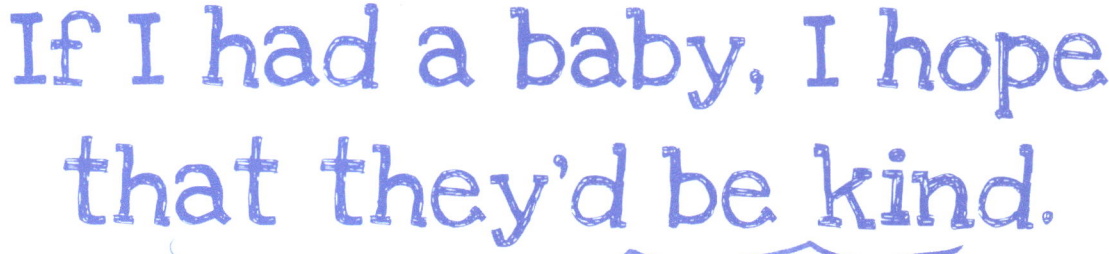

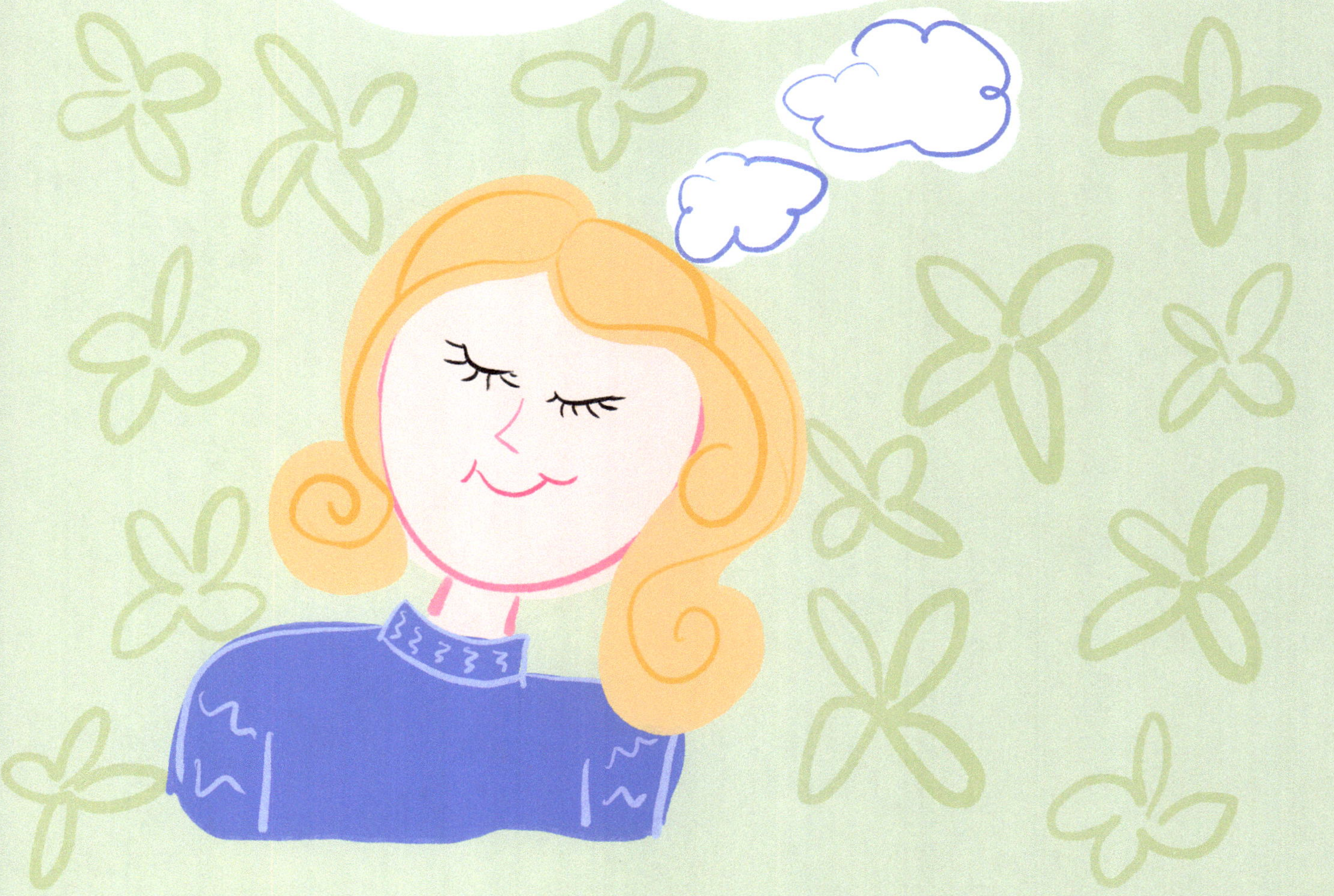

I think that I'd show them off like treasure that you find!

I might take them to the park to see butterflies and birds,

and read them classic literature to teach them big new words.

I'd take them to museums full of history and art,

and do community service,
so we'd learn to play our part.

We'd plant lots of trees and flowers, for the bees and for the air,

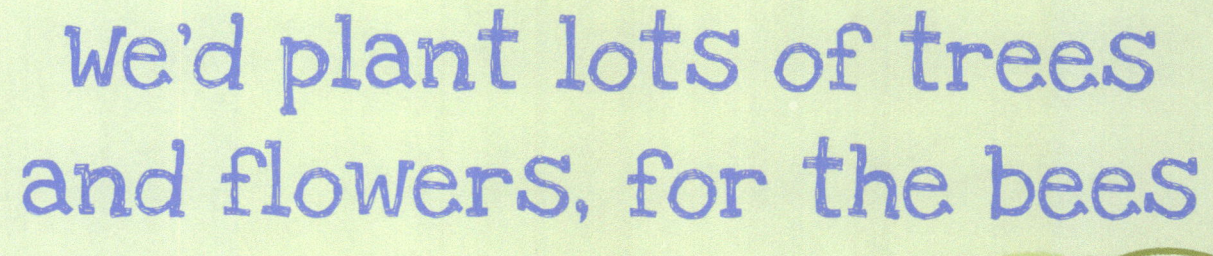

and if we knew someone was struggling, we'd show them how we care.

If I had a baby, I think we would have fun!

We might see bears and whales and even watch the horses run!

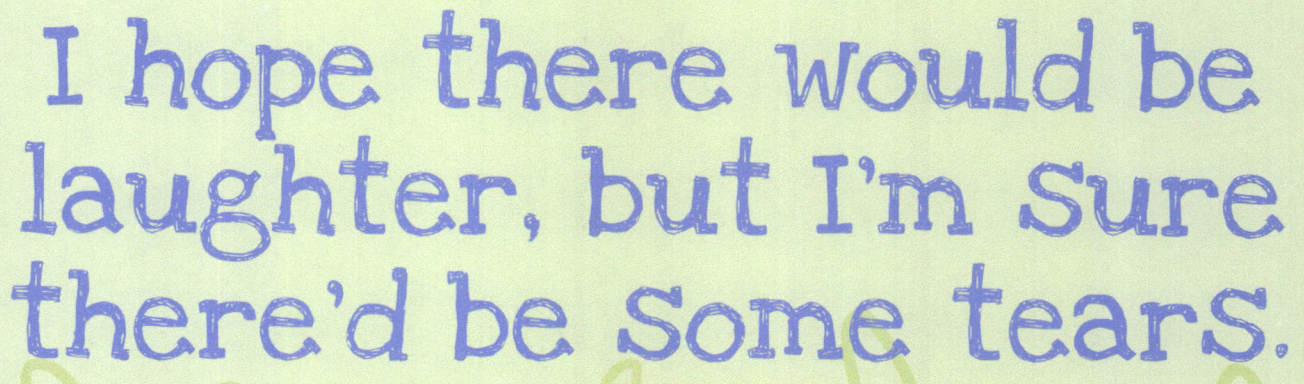
I hope there would be laughter, but I'm sure there'd be some tears.

Then I'd give them lots of snuggles and would quiet all their fears.

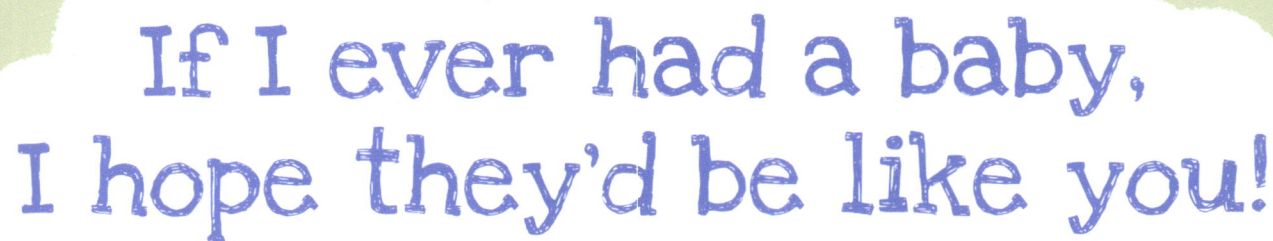

If I ever had a baby, I hope they'd be like you!

Alanna Grayce Campbell is an artist, adventurer, and fun aunt, residing on Florida's Gulf Coast. A born and raised Appalachian, she comes from a culture of creating and storytelling. Alanna and her sidekick, Wynn the Westie, spend their days imagining new worlds and experiencing this one. "If I Had a Baby" is her first published book as both author and illustrator.
Find more at www.alannagrayce.com

"If I Had A Baby" came to me as a nearly fully formed poem one evening as I contemplated my love for being the "fun aunt". "If I were to have a baby," I asked myself, "what would I want them to be like?" And so, this book is the result of that question. It's a daydream, meant to reflect any little one who might be seeing these pages.
I wanted every wee mind to know their value and to feel seen, represented, and loved.

www.ingramcontent.com/pod-product-compliance
Lightning Source LLC
Chambersburg PA
CBHW042055050526
44107CB00110B/1184